Romeo and Juliet

William Shakespeare

Saddleback's *Illustrated Classics*

ISBN: 978-1-56254-934-3
eBook: 978-1-60291-166-6

Printed in Malaysia
26 25 24 23 22   19 20 21 22 23

Welcome to
Saddleback's *Illustrated Classics*

We are proud to welcome you to Saddleback's *Illustrated Classics*. Saddleback's *Illustrated Classics* was designed specifically for the classroom to introduce readers to many of the great classics in literature. Each text, written and adapted by teachers and researchers, has been edited using the Dale-Chall vocabulary system. In addition, much time and effort has been spent to ensure that these high-interest stories retain all of the excitement, intrigue, and adventure of the original books.

With these graphically *Illustrated Classics*, you learn what happens in the story in a number of different ways. One way is by reading the words a character says. Another way is by looking at the drawings of the character. The artist can tell you what kind of person a character is and what he or she is thinking or feeling.

This series will help you to develop confidence and a sense of accomplishment as you finish each novel. The stories in Saddleback's *Illustrated Classics* are fun to read. And remember, fun motivates!

Overview

Everyone deserves to read the best literature our language has to offer. Saddleback's *Illustrated Classics* was designed to acquaint readers with the most famous stories from the world's greatest authors, while teaching essential skills. You will learn how to:

- Establish a purpose for reading
- Activate prior knowledge
- Evaluate your reading
- Listen to the language as it is written
- Extend literary and language appreciation through discussion and writing activities.

Reading is one of the most important skills you will ever learn. It provides the key to all kinds of information. By reading the *Illustrated Classics*, you will develop confidence and the self-satisfaction that comes from accomplishment—a solid foundation for any reader.

Step-By-Step

The following is a simple guide to using and enjoying each of your *Illustrated Classics*. To maximize your use of the learning activities provided, we suggest that you follow these steps:

1. *Listen!* We suggest that you listen to the read-along. (At this time, please ignore the beeps.) You will enjoy this wonderfully dramatized presentation.

2. *Post-reading Activities.* You have successfully read the story and listened to the audio presentation. Now answer the multiple-choice questions and other activities in the Study Guide.

Remember,

"Today's readers are tomorrow's leaders."

William Shakespeare

William Shakespeare was baptized on April 26, 1564, in Stratford-on-Avon, England, the third child of John Shakespeare, a well-to-do merchant, and Mary Arden, his wife. Young William probably attended the Stratford grammar school, where he learned English, Greek, and a great deal of Latin. Historians aren't sure of the exact date of Shakespeare's birth.

In 1582, Shakespeare married Anne Hathaway. By 1583 the couple had a daughter, Susanna, and two years later the twins, Hamnet and Judith. Somewhere between 1585 and 1592 Shakespeare went to London, where he became first an actor and then a playwright. His acting company, *The King's Men*, appeared most often in the *Globe* theater, a part of which Shakespeare himself owned.

In all, Shakespeare is believed to have written thirty-seven plays, several nondramatic poems, and a number of sonnets. In 1611 when he left the active life of the theater, he returned to Stratford and became a country gentleman, living in the second-largest house in town. For five years he lived a quiet life. Then, on April 23, 1616, William Shakespeare died and was buried in Trinity Church in Stratford. From his own time to the present, Shakespeare is considered one of the greatest writers of the English-speaking world.

William Shakespeare

Romeo and Juliet

ROMEO · Juliet · LORD & LADY MONTAGUE · FRIAR LAURENCE · LORD & LADY CAPULET · MERCUTIO · PRINCE ESCALUS · TYBALT

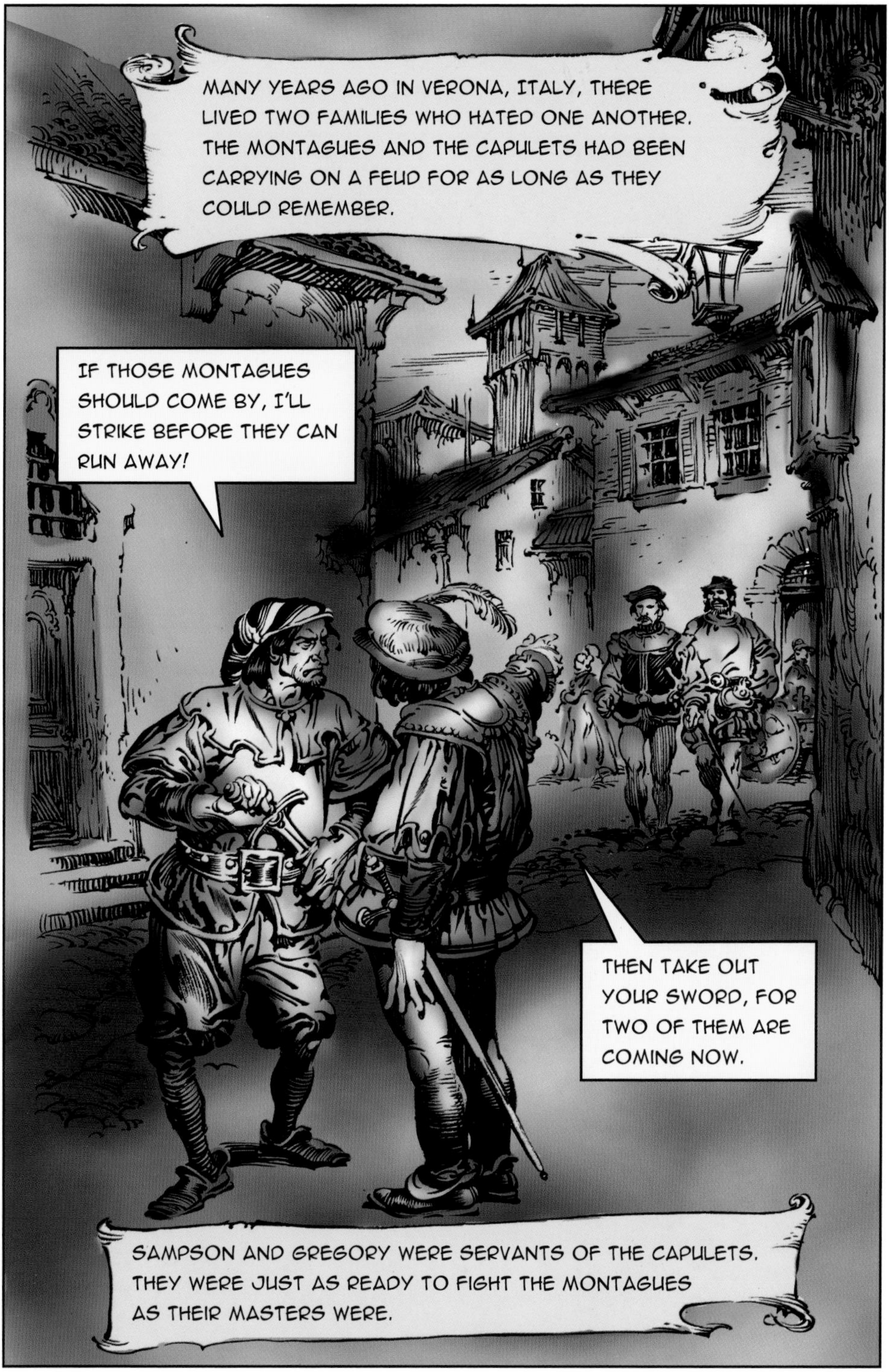
MANY YEARS AGO IN VERONA, ITALY, THERE LIVED TWO FAMILIES WHO HATED ONE ANOTHER. THE MONTAGUES AND THE CAPULETS HAD BEEN CARRYING ON A FEUD FOR AS LONG AS THEY COULD REMEMBER.
IF THOSE MONTAGUES SHOULD COME BY, I'LL STRIKE BEFORE THEY CAN RUN AWAY!
THEN TAKE OUT YOUR SWORD, FOR TWO OF THEM ARE COMING NOW.
SAMPSON AND GREGORY WERE SERVANTS OF THE CAPULETS. THEY WERE JUST AS READY TO FIGHT THE MONTAGUES AS THEIR MASTERS WERE.

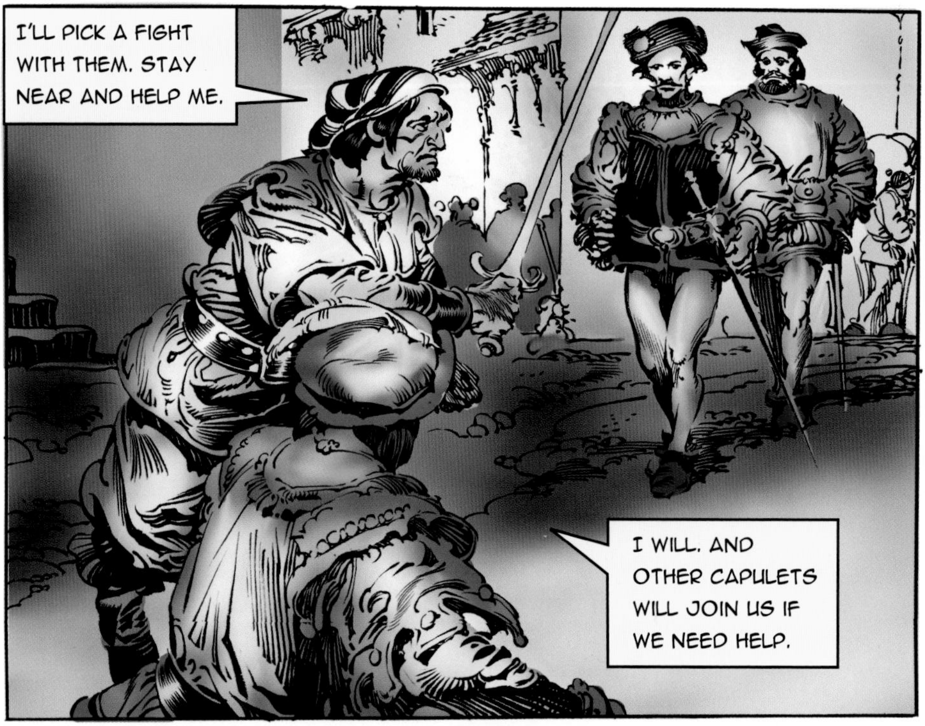
I'LL PICK A FIGHT WITH THEM. STAY NEAR AND HELP ME.
I WILL. AND OTHER CAPULETS WILL JOIN US IF WE NEED HELP.

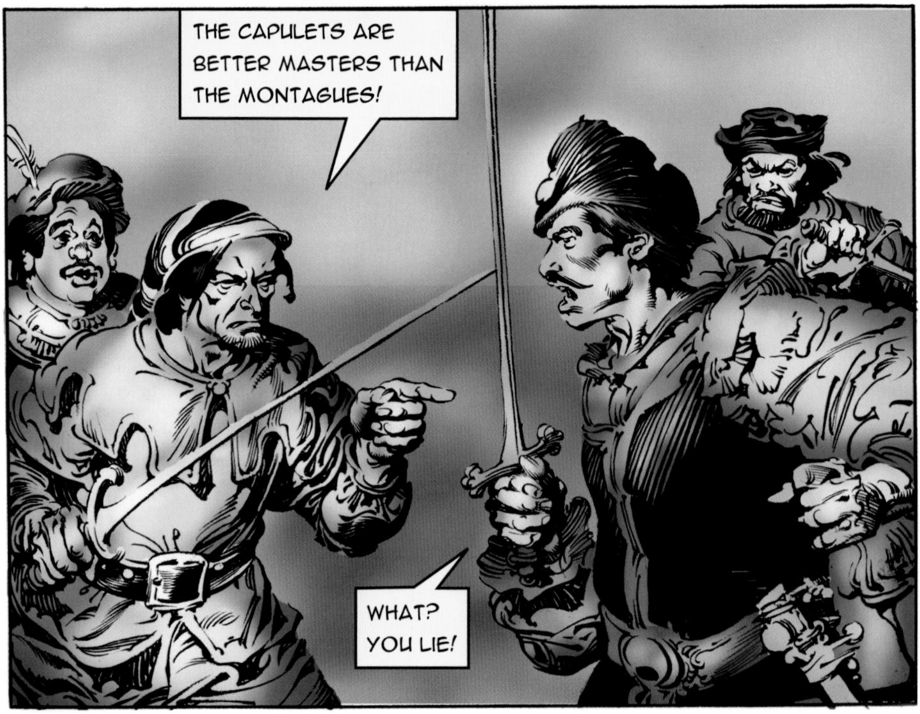
THE CAPULETS ARE BETTER MASTERS THAN THE MONTAGUES!
WHAT? YOU LIE!

AS THE SERVANTS PREPARED TO FIGHT, MONTAGUE'S NEPHEW, BENVOLIO, RUSHED UP TO THEM.

STOP, YOU FOOLS! YOU DON'T KNOW WHAT YOU'RE DOING!

JUST THEN TYBALT, A NEPHEW OF CAPULET'S WIFE, SAW BENVOLIO WITH HIS SWORD DRAWN. HE THOUGHT BENVOLIO WANTED TO FIGHT ALONG WITH THE SERVANTS.

WHY FIGHT THEM WHEN YOU CAN FIGHT ME, BENVOLIO?

I AM TRYING TO KEEP PEACE, TYBALT. IF YOU MUST USE YOUR SWORD, HELP ME TO SEPARATE THESE SERVANTS.

I DO NOT LIKE THE WORD PEACE. I HATE YOU AND ALL THE OTHER MONTAGUES. FIGHT ME, I SAY!

I SHALL BE THE DEATH OF YOU, BENVOLIO.

MANY GOOD CITIZENS OF VERONA WERE TIRED OF THE LONG FEUD. THEY RUSHED UP TO THE FIGHTING MEN.

STOP THEM, CITIZENS! STRIKE! BEAT THEM DOWN!

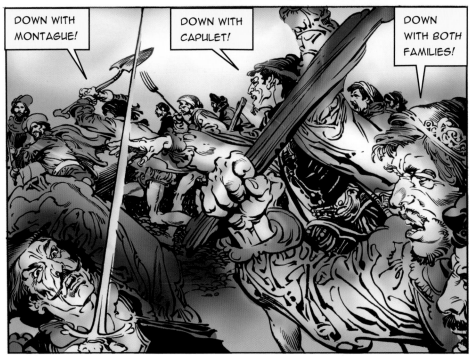

DOWN WITH MONTAGUE!

DOWN WITH CAPULET!

DOWN WITH *BOTH* FAMILIES!

HEARING THE NOISE, OLD CAPULET AND LORD MONTAGUE CAME OUT OF THEIR HOUSES TO SEE WHAT WAS HAPPENING.

LOOK! HERE COMES MONTAGUE WITH A SWORD. GET MINE FOR ME, WIFE.

NO. YOU ARE TOO OLD TO FIGHT.

THERE IS OLD CAPULET. LET GO OF ME WOMAN!

I WILL NOT!

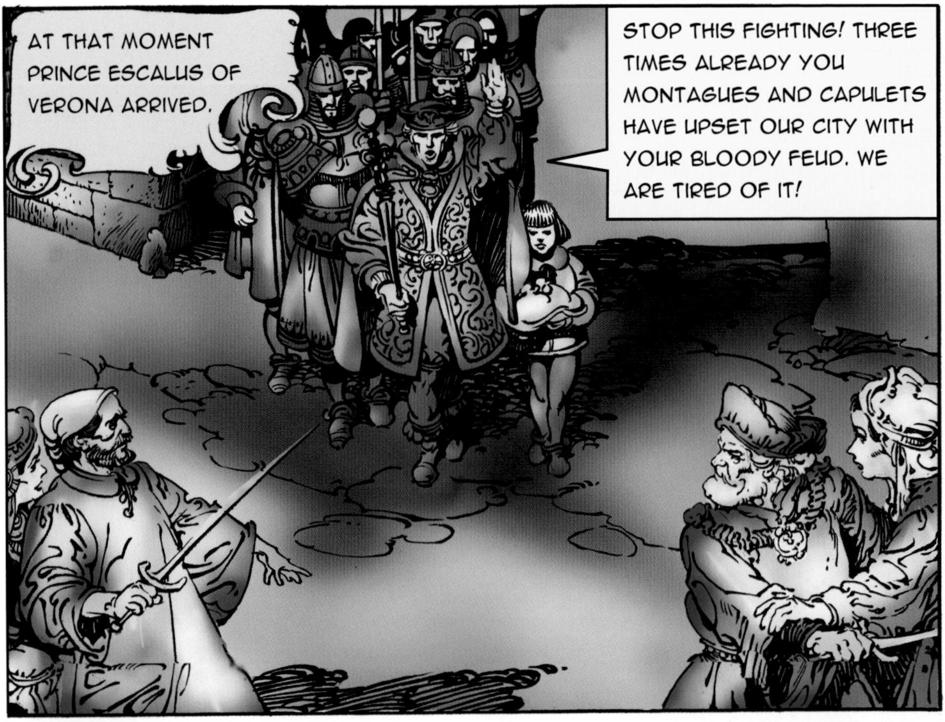
AT THAT MOMENT PRINCE ESCALUS OF VERONA ARRIVED.
STOP THIS FIGHTING! THREE TIMES ALREADY YOU MONTAGUES AND CAPULETS HAVE UPSET OUR CITY WITH YOUR BLOODY FEUD. WE ARE TIRED OF IT!

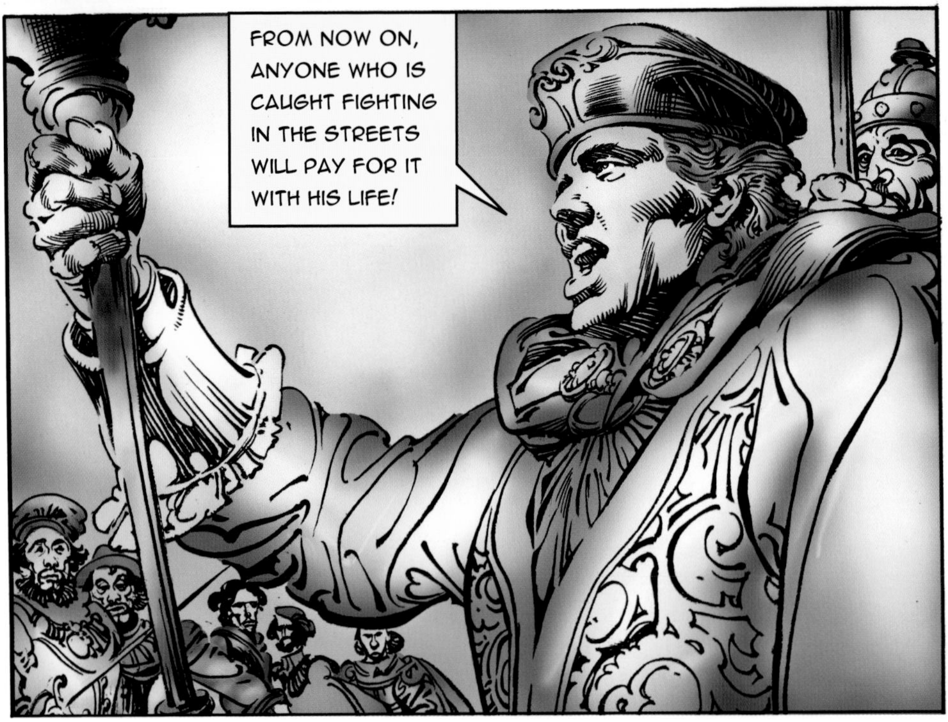
FROM NOW ON, ANYONE WHO IS CAUGHT FIGHTING IN THE STREETS WILL PAY FOR IT WITH HIS LIFE!

WITH THIS, THE PRINCE LEFT AND THE PEOPLE WENT BACK TO THEIR HOMES.

BY THE WAY, BEN-VOLIO, HAVE YOU SEEN MY SON ROMEO TODAY? I AM GLAD HE WAS NOT IN THIS FIGHT.

I SAW HIM WALKING THIS MORNING, LADY MONTAGUE. HE WANTED TO BE LEFT ALONE.

HE HAS BEEN DOING THAT A LOT LATELY, DEAR WIFE. HE STAYS UP ALL NIGHT LONG. AND DURING THE DAY HE LOCKS HIMSELF IN HIS ROOM.

AS THE SPOKE, ROMEO CAME DOWN THE STREET. BENVOLIO WENT ALONE TO TALK WITH HIM.

GOOD MORNING, COUSIN. WHAT IS BOTHERING YOU?

OH, BENVOLIO, I AM IN LOVE!

BUT THE GIRL I LOVE DOES NOT LOVE ME. IT TROUBLES MY HEART.

WHO IS SHE, ROMEO?

A WOMAN WHO SAYS THAT SHE WILL NEVER MARRY.

THEN FORGET HER AND FIND SOMEONE ELSE.

THERE ARE MANY OTHER LOVELY GIRLS IN VERONA.

NO ONE IS AS LOVELY A SHE IS. I CANNOT FORGET HER! GOOD-BYE, COUSIN.

POOR ROMEO! I MUST HELP HIM SOMEHOW!

A SHORT TIME LATER, OLD CAPULET MET WITH THE COUNTY PARIS, A HANDSOME AND RICH YOUNG MAN.

SIR, I WOULD LIKE TO MARRY YOUR DAUGHTER JULIET.

SHE IS VERY YOUNG. BUT IF SHE IS WILLING, I WILL LET YOU MARRY HER.

COME TO MY FEAST TONIGHT. YOU MAY SEE SOME OTHER LADY MORE BEAUTIFUL THAN JULIET.

I WILL COME, SIR.

OLD CAPULET CALLED HIS SERVANT AND GAVE HIM A LIST OF NAMES.

GO AND INVITE ALL THE PEOPLE ON THIS LIST TO MY HOME TONIGHT.

AT HIS MASTER'S ORDER, THE SERVANT TOOK THE LIST AND LEFT. BUT BECAUSE HE COULD NOT READ, HE HAD TO STOP SOMEONE AND ASK FOR HELP. AS LUCK WOULD HAVE IT, ROMEO AND BENVOLIO HAPPENED TO BE WALKING BY JUST THEN.

EXCUSE ME, GOOD SIRS. CAN YOU TELL ME WHOSE NAMES ARE ON THIS PAPER?

AS ROMEO READ THE LIST FOR HIM, HE SAW THAT THE NAME OF THE LADY HE LOVED WAS INCLUDED.

THANK YOU FOR HELPING ME, SIRS. MY MASTER IS LORD CAPULET. IF YOU ARE NOT MONTAGUES YOU ARE WELCOME TO ATTEND HIS PARTY.

WHEN THE SERVANT LEFT, BENVOLIO QUICKLY SPOKE WITH ROMEO.

SO YOUR LADY IS ON THE LIST! LET US GO TO THE FEAST TONIGHT. I AM SURE YOU WILL SEE OTHERS THERE WHO ARE JUST AS PRETTY. WHEN YOU COMPARE THEM, YOU WILL AGREE WITH ME!

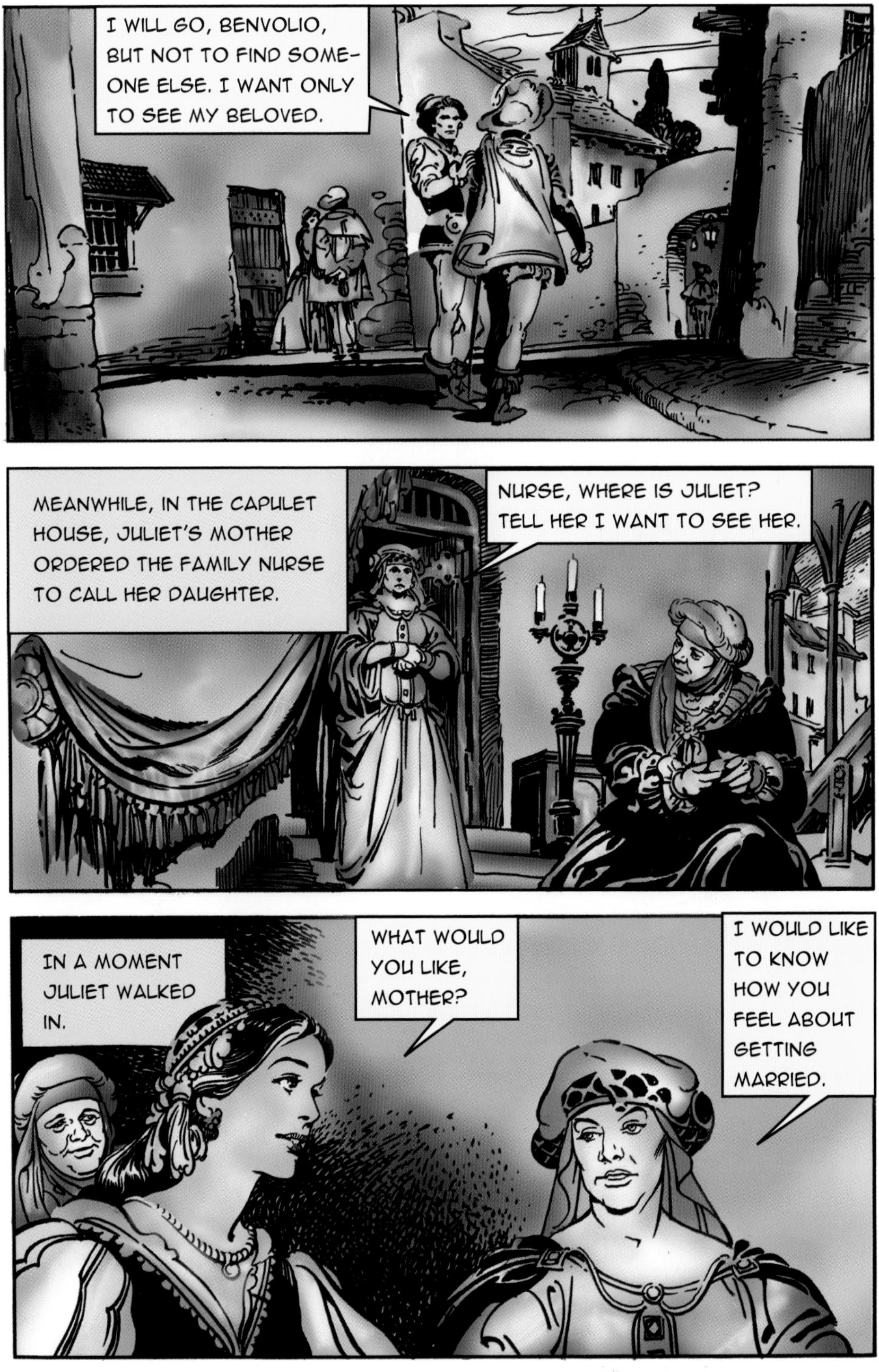
I WILL GO, BENVOLIO, BUT NOT TO FIND SOME-ONE ELSE. I WANT ONLY TO SEE MY BELOVED.
MEANWHILE, IN THE CAPULET HOUSE, JULIET'S MOTHER ORDERED THE FAMILY NURSE TO CALL HER DAUGHTER.
NURSE, WHERE IS JULIET? TELL HER I WANT TO SEE HER.
IN A MOMENT JULIET WALKED IN.
WHAT WOULD YOU LIKE, MOTHER?
I WOULD LIKE TO KNOW HOW YOU FEEL ABOUT GETTING MARRIED.

MARRIAGE? I HAVEN'T THOUGHT ABOUT IT.

WELL, THINK ABOUT IT NOW. MANY LADIES IN VERONA YOUNGER THAN YOURSELF ARE ALREADY MARRIED.

COUNTY PARIS HAS ASKED FOR YOUR HAND. HE WILL BE AT THE FEAST TONIGHT. DO YOU THINK YOU CAN LOVE HIM?

I WILL NOT KNOW UNTIL I SEE HIM, MOTHER.

NOT LONG AFTER-WARD, A SERVANT APPEARED AT THE DOOR.

MADAM, THE GUESTS HAVE ARRIVED, AND SUPPER WILL BE SERVED SOON.

WE'LL BE RIGHT THERE. JULIET, PARIS IS WAITING. LET US GO.

THAT EVENING ROMEO AND BENVOLIO JOINED THE OTHER GUESTS AT THE CAPULETS' COSTUME PARTY. MERCUTIO, ANOTHER FRIEND, WENT ALONG AS WELL.

CHEER UP, ROMEO. WHAT'S THE MATTER?

I HAD A BAD DREAM LAST NIGHT, MERCUTIO. I THINK IT WAS A WARNING.

COME ON. IF WE WASTE OUR TIME TALKING, WE WILL BE LATE FOR SUPPER.

IT DOESN'T MATTER, BENVOLIO.

I CANNOT SHAKE THIS FEELING THAT SOMETHING BAD IS GOING TO HAPPEN!

INSIDE THE HOUSE, LORD CAPULET GREETED THE MASKED GUESTS.

WELCOME, GENTLEMEN. WE MUST HAVE DANCING! PLAY, MUSICIANS, PLAY!

SOME TIME LATER, ROMEO ARRIVED. CATCHING SIGHT OF JULIET ACROSS THE ROOM, HE ASKED A SERVANT HER NAME.

WHAT LADY IS THAT? SHE IS VERY LOVELY.

I DO NOT KNOW HER NAME, SIR.

SHE IS LIKE A SNOWY DOVE AMONG DARK CROWS. MY HEART HAS NOT KNOWN LOVE UNTIL TONIGHT.

STANDING NEARBY, TYBALT HEARD ROMEO'S LOW WORDS AND RECOGNIZED HIS VOICE.

THIS MAN IS A MONTAGUE. WHERE IS MY SWORD?

WHY DO YOU SHOUT SO, TYBALT?

UNCLE, THAT MAN IS ROMEO, A MONTAGUE. HE HAS COME HERE TO RUIN YOUR PARTY.

THE CITIZENS OF VERONA THINK HIGHLY OF YOUNG ROMEO. I DO NOT WANT TROUBLE UNDER MY ROOF, TYBALT.

BAH! YOU SHOULD NOT ALLOW A MONTAGUE HERE. AS YOU WISH, I WILL NOT FIGHT HIM NOW. BUT SOON HE WILL HAVE TO PAY FOR THIS!

WHILE TYBALT ARGUED WITH OLD CAPULET, ROMEO WENT OVER TO SPEAK WITH JULIET.

MAY I TAKE YOUR HAND?

WHY NOT? SAINTS KISS BY HOLDING HANDS.

IF HANDS CAN KISS, MAY MY LIPS DO THE SAME?

AT THAT MOMENT, ROMEO AND JULIET FELL DEEPLY IN LOVE WITH ONE ANOTHER.

THEN JULIET'S NURSE DREW NEAR.

MADAM, YOUR MOTHER WOULD LIKE TO SPEAK WITH YOU.

VERY WELL.

AFTER JULIET LEFT, ROMEO TURNED TO THE NURSE.

WHO *IS* HER MOTHER?

WHY, SHE IS THE LADY OF THIS HOUSE.

HER MOTHER IS A CAPULET. THIS YOUNG GIRL IS AN ENEMY OF MY FAMILY. BUT I SHALL SURELY DIE WITHOUT HER!

COMING UP BEHIND HIM, BENVOLIO COULD TELL THAT SOMETHING HAD DISTURBED ROMEO.

AS THEY WALKED TO THE DOOR, LORD CAPULET URGED ROMEO AND BENVOLIO TO STAY. THEY REFUSED.

LET US LEAVE NOW.

YES, PERHAPS YOU ARE RIGHT.

WE MUST BE GOING, GOOD SIR. BUT WE ARE GLAD WE CAME.

WHEN THE YOUNG MEN HAD LEFT, CAPULET REALIZED THAT THE PARTY HAD GONE ON LONG ENOUGH.

THE HOUR GROWS LATE AND I MUST REST. THANK YOU FOR COMING, EVERYONE. GOOD NIGHT.

AS THE OTHER GUESTS WERE LEAVING, JULIET ASKED HER NURSE THE NAME OF THE YOUNG MAN SHE HAD LAST SPOKEN TO.

THE YOUNG MAN WHO KISSED YOU? HE IS A MONTAGUE. HIS NAME IS ROMEO, THE ONLY SON OF YOUR GREAT ENEMY.

MY ONLY LOVE SPRINGS FROM MY FAMILY'S HATE!

JULIET!

COME, GIRL. THE GUESTS HAVE ALL GONE, AND SOMEONE CALLS YOUR NAME.

MEANWHILE, ONCE OUTSIDE, ROMEO COULD NOT BEAR TO GO HOME WITHOUT CATCHING ANOTHER GLIMPSE OF HIS BELOVED JULIET.

HOW CAN I GO FORWARD WHEN MY LOVE REMAINS HERE?

I MUST SEE JULIET AGAIN!

AS ROMEO DISAPPEARED OVER THE GARDEN WALL, BENVOLIO AND MERCUTIO CAME LOOKING FOR HIM.

HE RAN THIS WAY. CALL HIM, MERCUTIO.

I DID, BENVOLIO. BUT HE WON'T ANSWER ME.

LET'S GO THEN, MERCUTIO. WE CAN'T FIND SOMEONE WHO DOESN'T WISH TO BE FOUND.

MEANWHILE, IN THE GARDEN, ROMEO SAW JULIET AT HER BALCONY WINDOW.

WAIT! WHAT LIGHT IS THAT? IT IS JULIET, AS BRIGHT AND BEAUTIFUL AS THE SUN!

WITHOUT SEEING ROMEO, JULIET STEPPED OUT ONTO THE BALCONY AND SPOKE QUIETLY TO HERSELF.

OH, ROMEO, IF ONLY YOU WERE NOT A MONTAGUE! YET, IF YOU WON'T CHANGE, I'LL DENY MY NAME AND NO LONGER BE A CAPULET.

IT IS ONLY THE MONTAGUE NAME THAT MAKES ROMEO AN ENEMY. TAKE THAT AWAY, AND I WOULD MARRY HIM!

AT THIS, ROMEO SPOKE UP.

I WILL HOLD YOU TO YOUR WORD, DEAR JULIET.

ROMEO! HOW DID YOU GET HERE? THIS HOUSE MEANS DEATH FOR YOU.

IF MY RELATIVES FIND YOU HERE, THEY'LL MURDER YOU!

I WOULD RATHER END MY LIFE FROM YOUR FAMILY'S HATE, JULIET, THAN DIE WITHOUT YOUR LOVE!

ROMEO AND JULIET SPOKE FOR A FEW MOMENTS OF THEIR LOVE. THEN JULIET HEARD HER NURSE CALLING AT THE BEDROOM DOOR.

GOOD NIGHT, MY LOVE.

I MUST GO. IF YOUR LOVE FOR ME IS TRUE, TELL MY SERVANT TOMORROW WHEN I SEND HIM TO YOU. THEN I SHALL MARRY YOU.

I WILL WAIT FOR HIM AT NINE O'CLOCK IN THE MORNING.

ROMEO CLIMBED BACK OVER THE WALL. EVEN THOUGH IT WAS VERY LATE, HE KNEW HE WOULD NOT BE ABLE TO SLEEP.

I WILL GO TO SEE FRIAR LAURENCE AND TELL HIM WHAT HAS HAPPENED.

ROMEO, YOU ARE UP EARLY THIS MORNING. WHY, I THINK YOU HAVEN'T BEEN TO BED AT ALL!

THAT IS RIGHT, FATHER. EVEN SO, I'VE HAD A SWEETER REST THAN YOU HAVE!

HAVE YOU BEEN WITH ROSALINE?

NO. I HAVE COMPLETELY FORGOTTEN HER.

WHERE HAVE YOU BEEN, THEN?

I HAVE FALLEN IN LOVE WITH JULIET, LORD CAPULET'S DAUGHTER. YOU MUST MARRY US!

AFTER A FEW MOMENTS OF SILENCE, FRIAR LAURENCE AGREED.

I WILL HELP YOU, ROMEO. BY JOINING THE MONTAGUES AND THE CAPULETS, I MAY END THE FEUD BETWEEN YOUR TWO FAMILIES!

EARLY THE NEXT MORNING, BENVOLIO AND MERCUTIO WALKED THE STREETS OF VERONA SEARCHING FOR ROMEO.

I SPOKE WITH ROMEO'S FATHER. HE DID NOT COME HOME LAST NIGHT.

WHERE CAN HE BE?

TYBALT WAS ANGRY THAT ROMEO WENT TO THE PARTY. HE SENT A LETTER TO ROMEO'S HOUSE.

IT'S A CHALLENGE, I'LL BET!

AND ROMEO WILL FIGHT.

ROMEO IS AS GOOD AS DEAD. IF CUPID'S ARROW DOESN'T KILL HIM, TYBALT'S SWORD WILL.

BENVOLIO WAS THE FIRST TO SEE HIS FRIEND COMING TOWARD THEM.

AH, HERE COMES ROMEO.

GOOD DAY TO YOU BOTH. PLEASE FORGIVE ME FOR RUNNING OFF WITHOUT YOU LAST NIGHT.

JUST THEN JULIET'S NURSE AND A SERVANT WALKED UP.

CAN ANY OF YOU GENTLEMEN TELL ME WHERE I MIGHT FIND ROMEO?

I AM ROMEO.

I WOULD LIKE TO SPEAK WITH YOU IN PRIVATE, SIR.

AT THIS, MERCUTIO AND BENVOLIO EXCUSED THEMSELVES.

WE ARE GOING TO DINNER AT YOUR FATHER'S HOUSE, ROMEO.

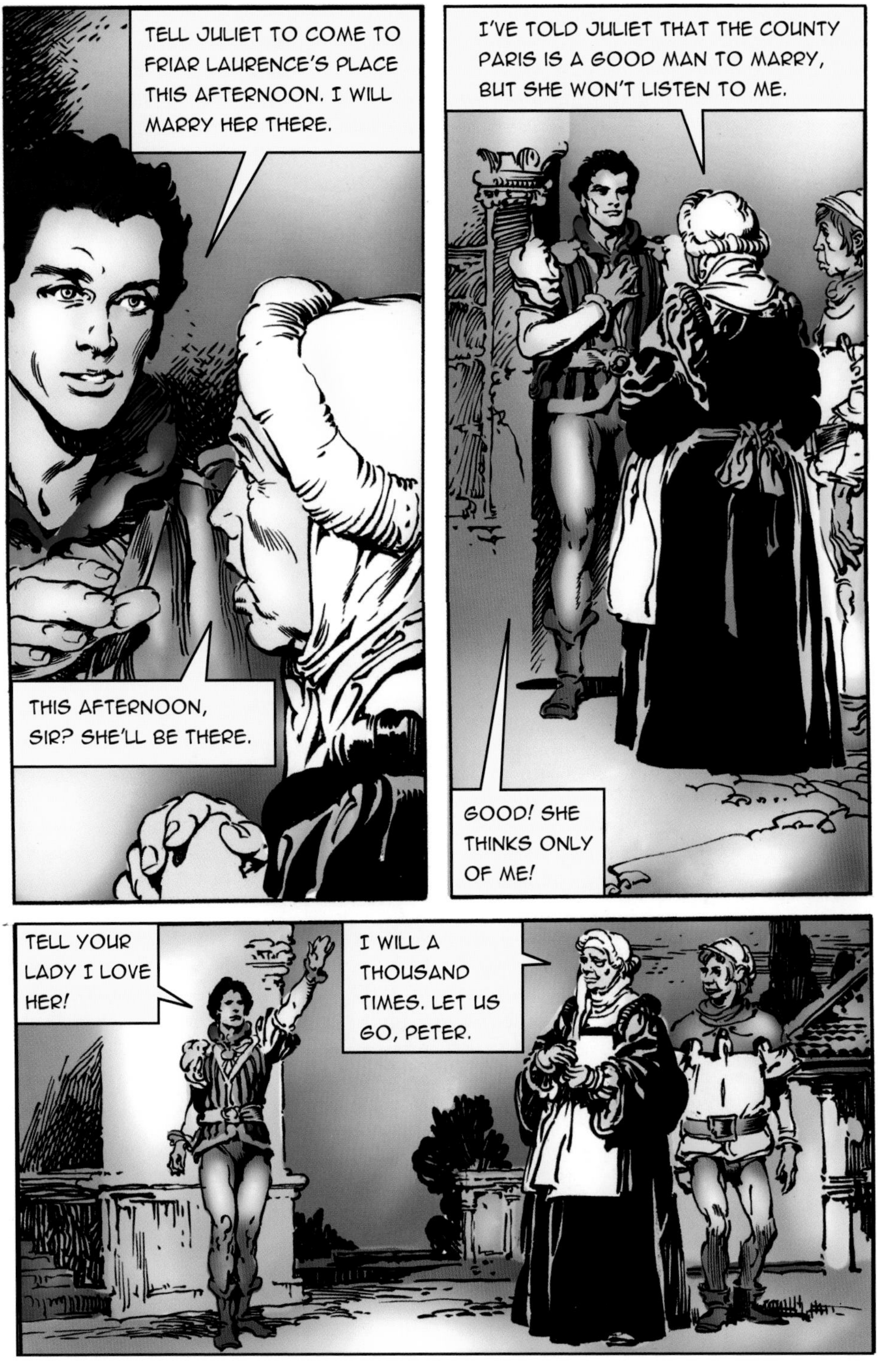
TELL JULIET TO COME TO FRIAR LAURENCE'S PLACE THIS AFTERNOON. I WILL MARRY HER THERE.
THIS AFTERNOON, SIR? SHE'LL BE THERE.
I'VE TOLD JULIET THAT THE COUNTY PARIS IS A GOOD MAN TO MARRY, BUT SHE WON'T LISTEN TO ME.
GOOD! SHE THINKS ONLY OF ME!
TELL YOUR LADY I LOVE HER!
I WILL A THOUSAND TIMES. LET US GO, PETER.

MEANWHILE, JULIET WAS WAITING IN HER GARDEN. THE NURSE HAD BEEN GONE FOR ABOUT THREE HOURS.

WHERE CAN SHE BE? SHE SAID SHE WOULD BE BACK IN HALF AN HOUR!

FINALLY THE NURSE APPEARED.

WHAT NEWS IS THERE? DID YOU MEET ROMEO?

ROMEO IS AT FRIAR LAURENCE'S PLACE. GO THERE, AND HE WILL MAKE YOU HIS WIFE.

AT THIS, JULIET HURRIED AWAY.

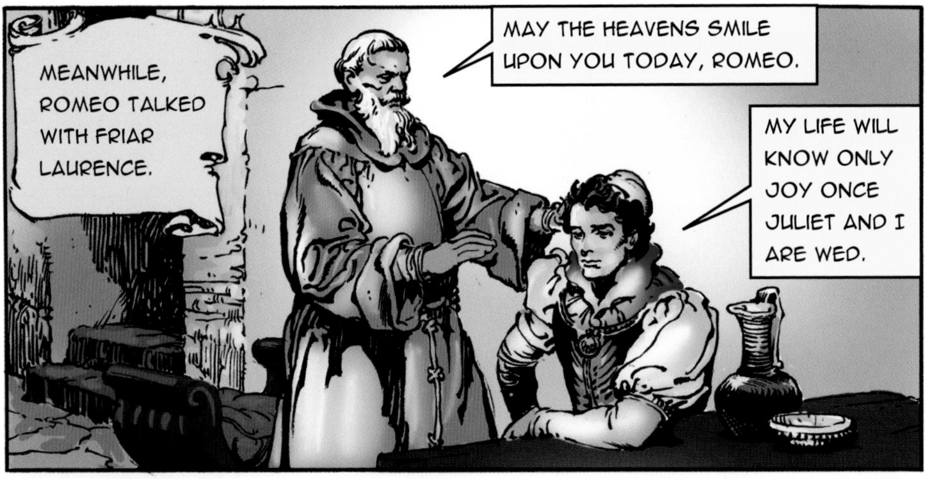
MEANWHILE, ROMEO TALKED WITH FRIAR LAURENCE.
MAY THE HEAVENS SMILE UPON YOU TODAY, ROMEO.
MY LIFE WILL KNOW ONLY JOY ONCE JULIET AND I ARE WED.

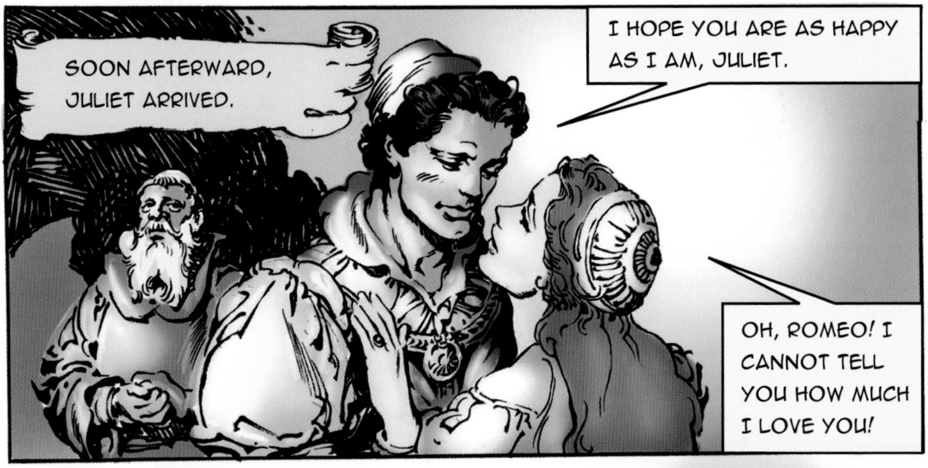
SOON AFTERWARD, JULIET ARRIVED.
I HOPE YOU ARE AS HAPPY AS I AM, JULIET.
OH, ROMEO! I CANNOT TELL YOU HOW MUCH I LOVE YOU!

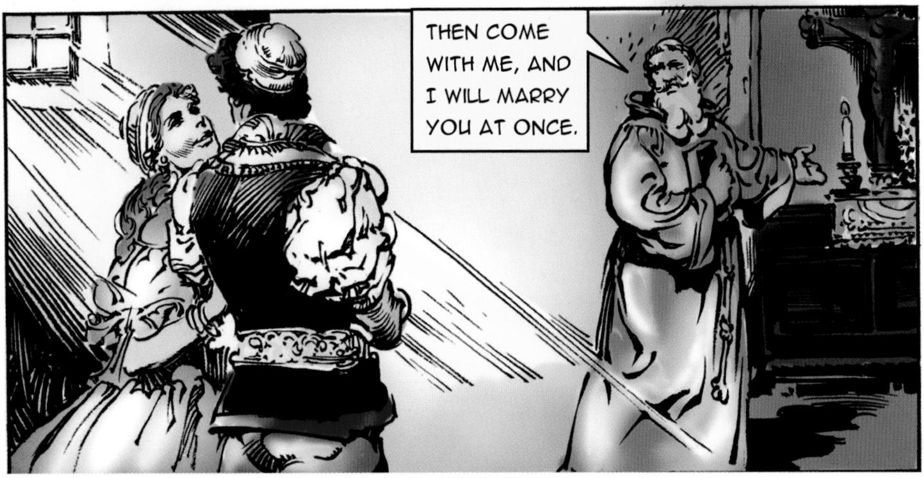
THEN COME WITH ME, AND I WILL MARRY YOU AT ONCE.

IT GREW VERY WARM THAT AFTERNOON, AND BENVOLIO PLEADED WITH MERCUTIO TO GO HOME.

I THINK WE SHOULD LEAVE, MERCUTIO. IT IS HOT, AND MANY CAPULETS ARE NEARBY. IF WE MEET ONE OF THEM, WE WILL SURELY BE IN FOR A FIGHT.

COME ON, NOW, BENVOLIO. YOU USE THE SMALLEST EXCUSE TO PICK A QUARREL YOURSELF!

AS THEY WERE SPEAKING, TYBALT AND SOME OTHER CAPULETS APPEARED. TYBALT WAS LOOKING FOR ROMEO.

HERE COME THE CAPULETS.

I DON'T CARE. LET THEM COME!

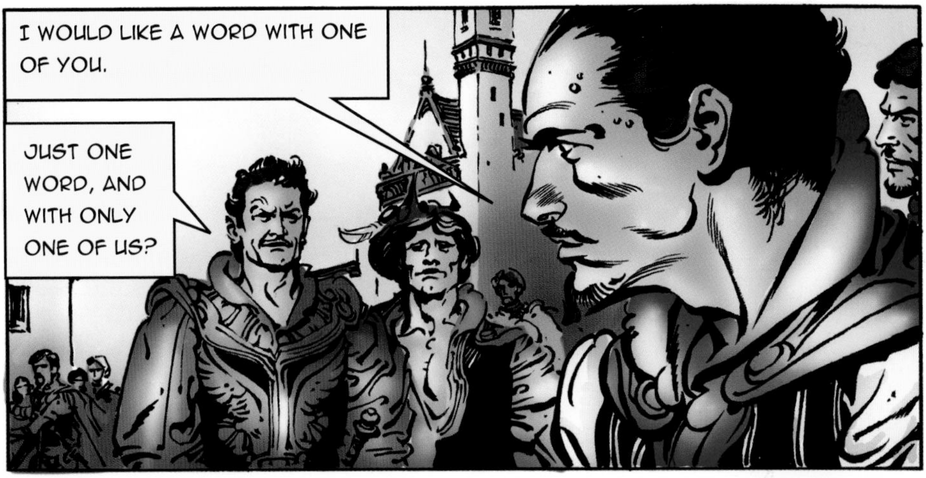
I WOULD LIKE A WORD WITH ONE OF YOU.
JUST ONE WORD, AND WITH ONLY ONE OF US?

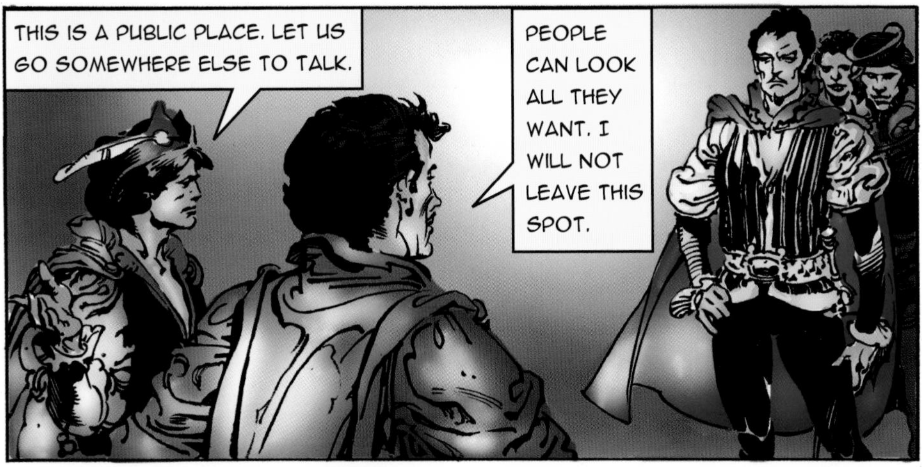
THIS IS A PUBLIC PLACE. LET US GO SOMEWHERE ELSE TO TALK.
PEOPLE CAN LOOK ALL THEY WANT. I WILL NOT LEAVE THIS SPOT.

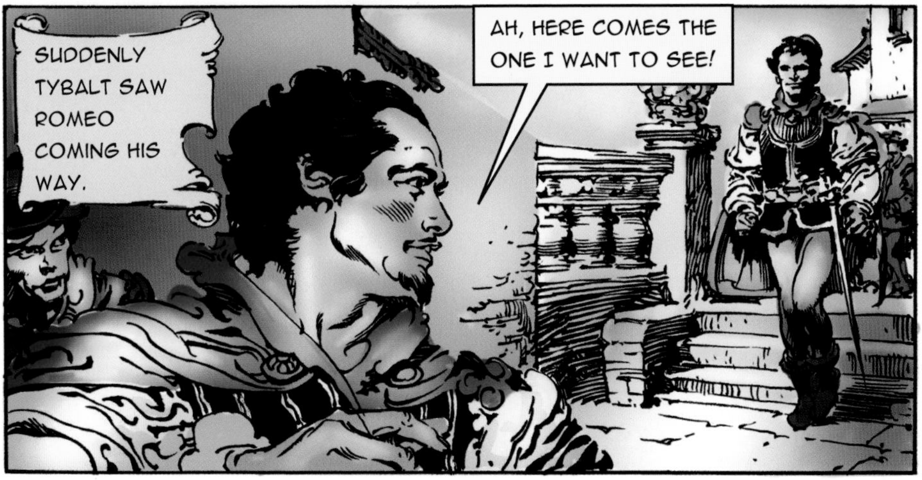
SUDDENLY TYBALT SAW ROMEO COMING HIS WAY.
AH, HERE COMES THE ONE I WANT TO SEE!

ROMEO HAD JUST BEEN MARRIED TO JULIET. TYBALT'S WORDS COULD NOT ANGER HIM.

YOU HAVE INSULTED ME, ROMEO. DRAW YOUR SWORD.

I CANNOT FIGHT YOU, TYBALT. THE CAPULET NAME IS AS DEAR AS MY OWN!

HEARING THIS, MERCUTIO THOUGHT ROMEO WAS TOO LOVE-SICK TO FIGHT. HE CHALLENGED TYBALT HIM-SELF.

I WILL FIGHT YOU, TYBALT. HURRY, BEFORE I CUT OFF YOUR EARS!

THEN I AM READY, MERCUTIO.

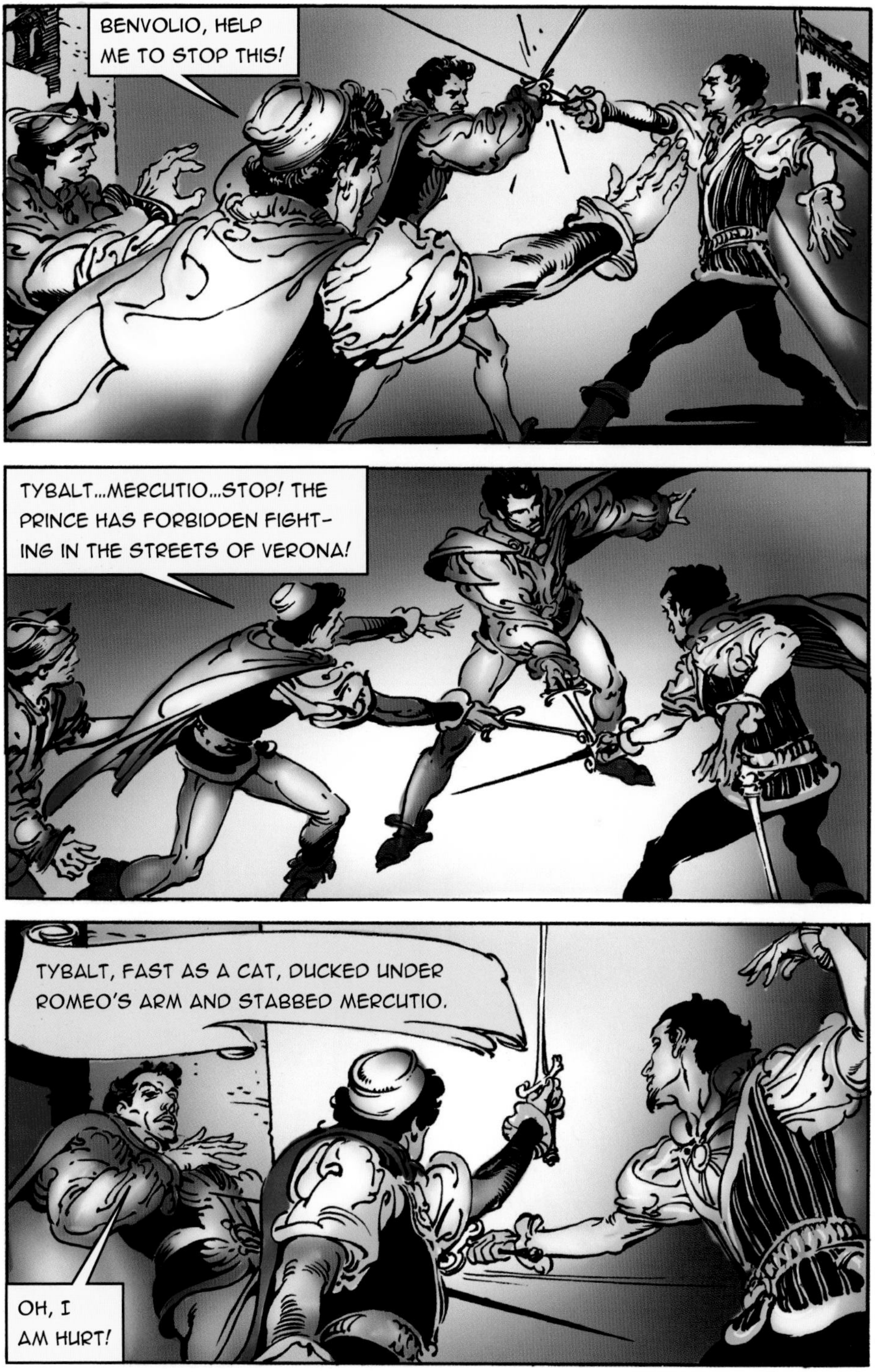
BENVOLIO, HELP ME TO STOP THIS!
TYBALT...MERCUTIO...STOP! THE PRINCE HAS FORBIDDEN FIGHTING IN THE STREETS OF VERONA!
TYBALT, FAST AS A CAT, DUCKED UNDER ROMEO'S ARM AND STABBED MERCUTIO.
OH, I AM HURT!

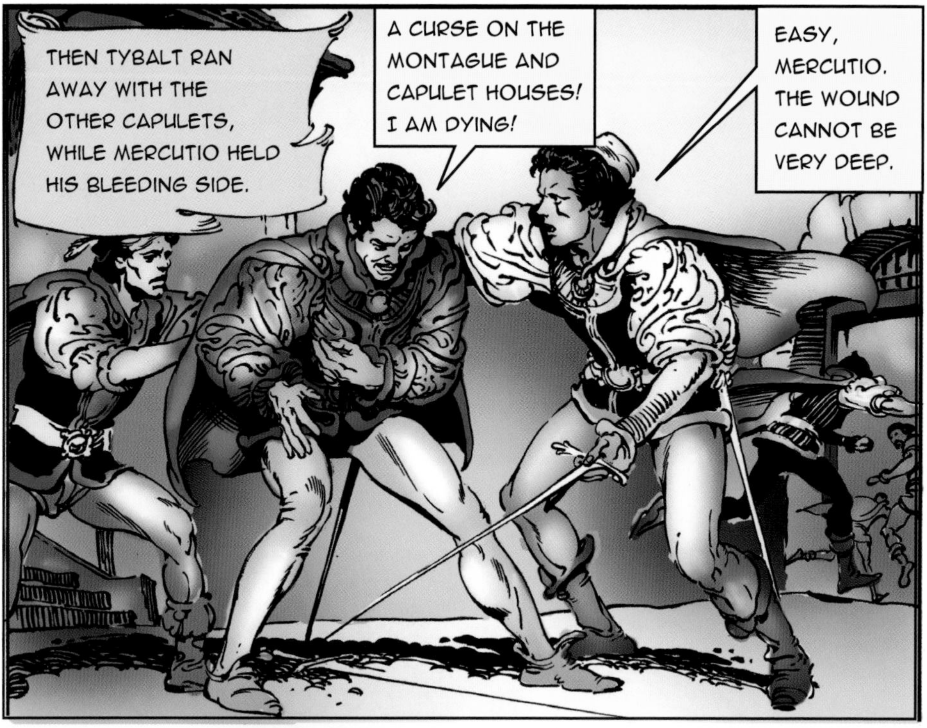
THEN TYBALT RAN AWAY WITH THE OTHER CAPULETS, WHILE MERCUTIO HELD HIS BLEEDING SIDE.
A CURSE ON THE MONTAGUE AND CAPULET HOUSES! I AM DYING!
EASY, MERCUTIO. THE WOUND CANNOT BE VERY DEEP.

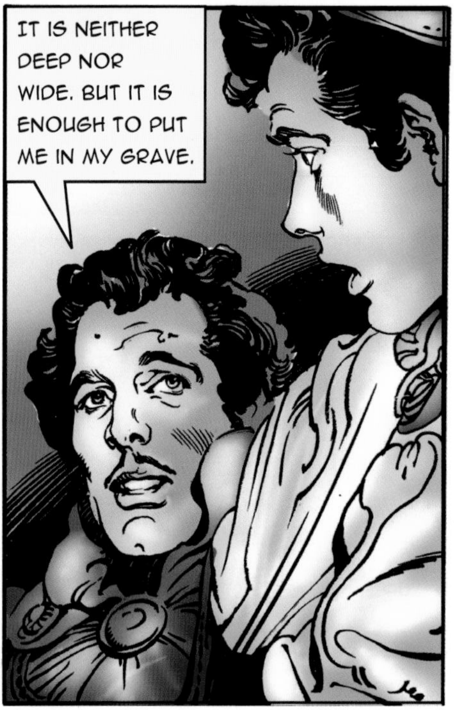
IT IS NEITHER DEEP NOR WIDE. BUT IT IS ENOUGH TO PUT ME IN MY GRAVE.

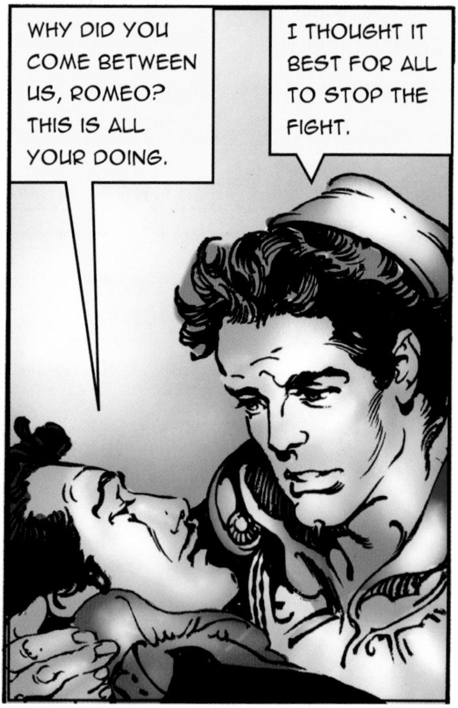
WHY DID YOU COME BETWEEN US, ROMEO? THIS IS ALL YOUR DOING.
I THOUGHT IT BEST FOR ALL TO STOP THE FIGHT.

HELP ME TO A HOUSE, BENVOLIO, OR I WILL DIE IN THE STREET.

POOR MERCUTIO! THIS IS ALL MY FAULT. HE WAS HURT TRYING TO PROTECT MY REPUTATION. AND I DIDN'T' WANT TO FIGHT TYBALT BECAUSE HE IS JULIET'S COUSIN.

JUST THEN BENVOLIO RUSHED OUT OF A NEARBY HOUSE.

ROMEO! BRAVE MERCUTIO IS DEAD!

THEN I MUST KILL TYBALT, OR BE KILLED MYSELF!

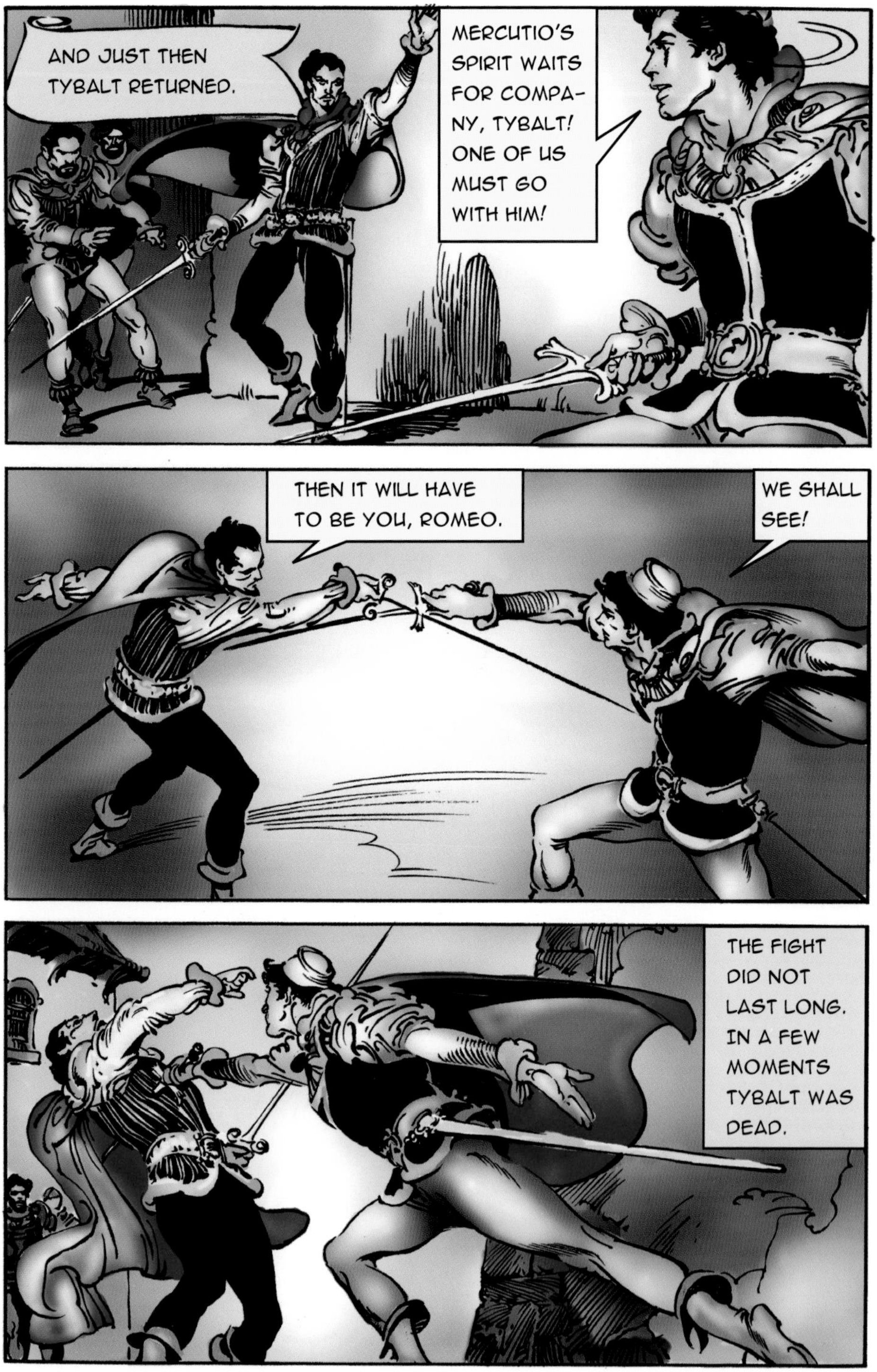
AND JUST THEN TYBALT RETURNED.
MERCUTIO'S SPIRIT WAITS FOR COMPANY, TYBALT! ONE OF US MUST GO WITH HIM!
THEN IT WILL HAVE TO BE YOU, ROMEO.
WE SHALL SEE!
THE FIGHT DID NOT LAST LONG. IN A FEW MOMENTS TYBALT WAS DEAD.

SEEING THIS, BENVOLIO URGED ROMEO TO LEAVE.

PEOPLE ARE COMING! YOU WILL GET THE DEATH PENALTY IF YOU ARE CAUGHT.

BENVOLIO IS RIGHT. I AM A FOOL.

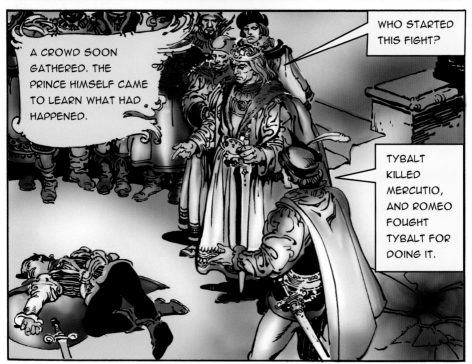

A CROWD SOON GATHERED. THE PRINCE HIMSELF CAME TO LEARN WHAT HAD HAPPENED.

WHO STARTED THIS FIGHT?

TYBALT KILLED MERCUTIO, AND ROMEO FOUGHT TYBALT FOR DOING IT.

AT THIS, LADY CAPULET SPOKE UP.

BENVOLIO IS A GOOD FRIEND OF THE MONTAGUES, GOOD PRINCE. DO NOT LISTEN TO HIS STORY.

BUT OLD MONTAGUE ANSWERED FOR HIS SON.

IF TYBALT KILLED MERCUTIO, THEN ROMEO WAS RIGHT IN KILLING TYBALT.

THE PRINCE LISTENED TO BOTH SIDES. THEN HE SPOKE.

ROMEO MUST BE SENT AWAY FROM VERONA. IF HE IS CAUGHT BEFORE LEAVING THE CITY, HE WILL BE PUT TO DEATH.

MEANWHILE, KNOWING NOTHING OF WHAT HAD HAPPENED, JULIET WAS SITTING QUIETLY IN HER GARDEN.

TONIGHT ROMEO WILL CLIMB MY BALCONY, AND WE WILL BE TOGETHER!

SUDDENLY THE NURSE ARRIVED CARRYING THE ROPE LADDER THAT ROMEO WOULD USE. SHE WAS VERY UPSET.

WHAT IS WRONG, NURSE?

TYBALT IS DEAD, KILLED BY ROMEO. THE PRINCE HAS SENT YOUR NEW HUSBAND AWAY FROM THE CITY!

AT THIS, JULIET WAS FILLED WITH GRIEF.

IF I CANNOT HAVE ROMEO, I WILL DIE!

NO, JULIET. DO NOT KILL YOURSELF. I KNOW WHERE ROMEO IS HIDING. I WILL TELL HIM TO SEE YOU TONIGHT BEFORE HE LEAVES.

MEANWHILE, FRIAR LAURENCE RETURNED TO HIS HOME WITH NEWS FOR ROMEO.

WHAT HAVE YOU LEARNED, FATHER?

PRINCE ESCALUS HAS GIVEN YOU A GENTLE PUNISHMENT. YOU ARE TO BE SENT AWAY FOREVER.

I WOULD RATHER DIE THAN BE SENT AWAY. HOW CAN I LIVE WITHOUT JULIET?

JUST THEN JULIET'S NURSE KNOCKED AND ENTERED.

ROMEO, I COME FROM LADY JULIET. SHE ASKS YOU TO COME AND COMFORT HER TONIGHT.

GO AND SEE JULIET, ROMEO. SOMEDAY PRINCE ESCALUS MAY PARDON YOU. THEN YOU CAN RETURN TO YOUR HOME.

FRIAR LAURENCE TOLD ROMEO TO LEAVE VE- RONA BEFORE DAWN AND GO TO THE CITY OF MANTUA TO LIVE.

JUST BE SURE TO LEAVE THE CITY BEFORE DAWN. GO TO MANTUA FOR THE TIME BEING, AND I WILL CONTACT YOU THROUGH YOUR SERVANT BALTHASAR. NOW GO.

THANK YOU, FATHER. FARE- WELL AND GOOD NIGHT.

ALL THIS TIME, JULIET'S FATHER DID NOT KNOW HIS DAUGHTER WAS WED TO ROMEO. HE MADE PLANS WITH THE COUNTY PARIS.

I WILL LET YOU MARRY JULIET. THEN SHE WILL FORGET ABOUT HER DEAD COUSIN.

YOU MAY TAKE MY DAUGHTER AS YOUR WIFE NEXT THURSDAY. HOW DOES THAT SOUND?

SIR, I WISH TOMORROW WERE THURSDAY!

AT THIS VERY MOMENT ROMEO WAS STANDING ON JULIET'S BALCONY.

MUST YOU GO SO SOON, ROMEO?

I WILL GO UPSTAIRS AND TELL JULIET ABOUT THIS.

YES, MY LOVE. THE BIRDS ARE STARTING TO SING AND THE SUN IS COMING UP. IF I STAY ANY LONGER I WILL BE KILLED.

BUT I WOULD GLADLY STAY AND DIE FOR YOU, JULIET, IF THAT IS WHAT YOU WISH.

NO, NO! YOU MUST LEAVE!

JUST THEN JULIET'S NURSE CALLED TO HER.

SHE MUST NOT FIND ME HERE! KISS ME, JULIET, AND I WILL GO.

MADAM, YOUR MOTHER IS COMING TO SEE YOU.

I WILL WAIT EVERY DAY FOR A MESSAGE FROM YOU!

AND I WILL SEND ONE, I PROMISE.

WITH THAT, ROMEO DISAPPEARED INTO THE GARDEN AND WAS GONE.

AS LADY CAPULET ENTERED THE ROOM, SHE SAW HOW SAD JULIET WAS AND THOUGHT SHE WAS STILL WEEPING AT TYBALT'S DEATH.

I HAVE GOOD NEW, JULIET. TO MAKE YOU HAPPY, WE HAVE ARRANGED FOR YOU TO MARRY THE COUNTY PARIS.

OH, NO! MOTHER, I WILL NEVER MARRY HIM!

IN A MOMENT HER FATHER ENTERED THE ROOM. LADY CAPULET TURNED TO HIM.

JULIET DOES NOT WANT TO MARRY PARIS.

WHAT? YOU SHALL, JULIET, OR I WILL SEND YOU OUT OF THIS HOUSE!

OF COURSE THE CAPULETS THOUGHT THEY KNEW WHAT WAS BEST FOR THEIR DAUGHTER. WHEN SHE WOULD NOT DO AS THEY WISHED, THEY LEFT HER ROOM ANGRILY. THEN JULIET FOUND A WAY TO GET OUT OF THE HOUSE.

NURSE, I MUST GO AND SEE FRIAR LAURENCE. I HAVE TO TELL HIM THAT I MADE MY PARENTS ANGRY.

THAT'S A GOOD IDEA, JULIET.

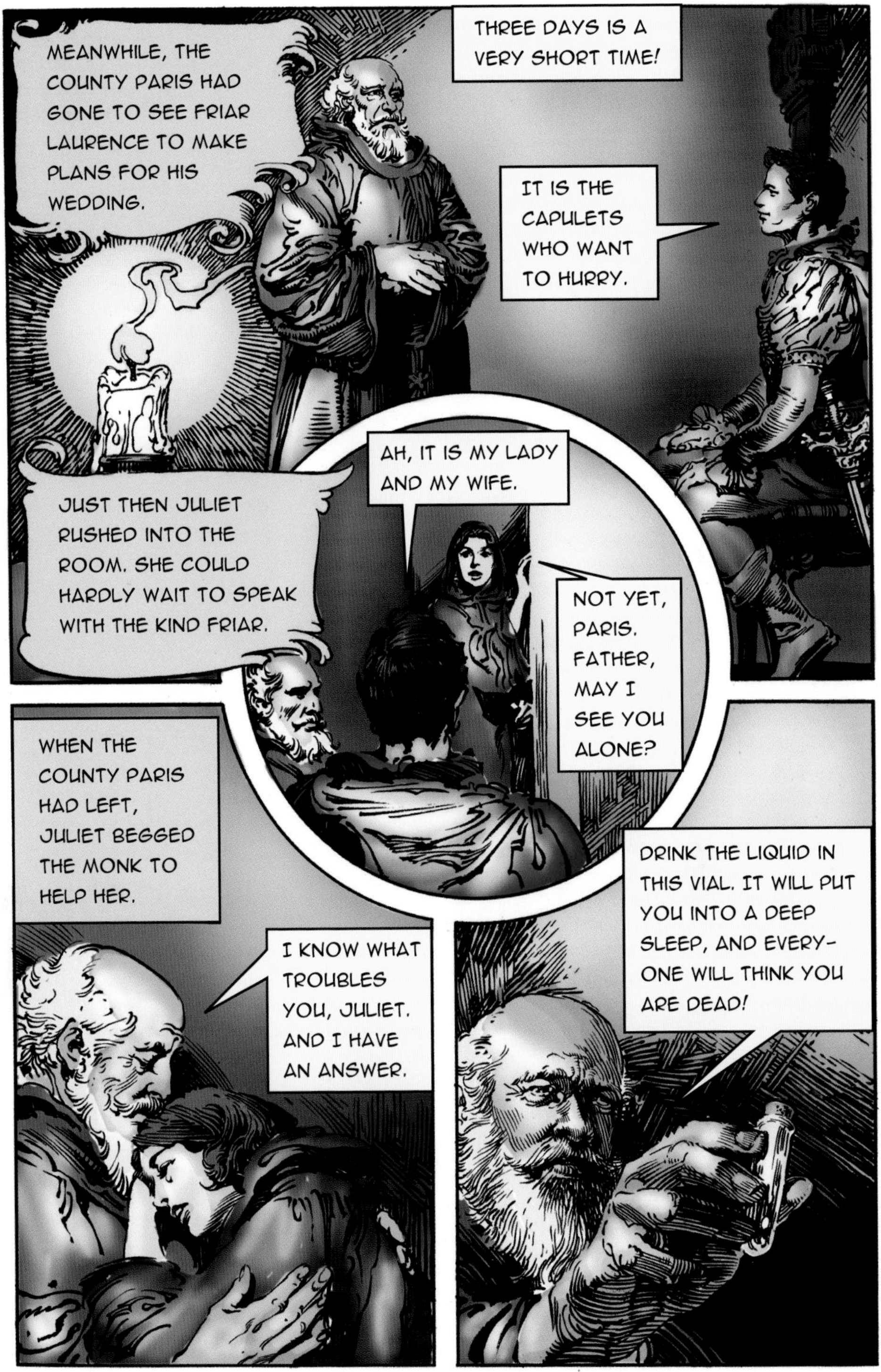
MEANWHILE, THE COUNTY PARIS HAD GONE TO SEE FRIAR LAURENCE TO MAKE PLANS FOR HIS WEDDING.
THREE DAYS IS A VERY SHORT TIME!
IT IS THE CAPULETS WHO WANT TO HURRY.
JUST THEN JULIET RUSHED INTO THE ROOM. SHE COULD HARDLY WAIT TO SPEAK WITH THE KIND FRIAR.
AH, IT IS MY LADY AND MY WIFE.
NOT YET, PARIS. FATHER, MAY I SEE YOU ALONE?
WHEN THE COUNTY PARIS HAD LEFT, JULIET BEGGED THE MONK TO HELP HER.
I KNOW WHAT TROUBLES YOU, JULIET. AND I HAVE AN ANSWER.
DRINK THE LIQUID IN THIS VIAL. IT WILL PUT YOU INTO A DEEP SLEEP, AND EVERY-ONE WILL THINK YOU ARE DEAD!

YOU WILL THEN BE PLACED IN A TOMB. I WILL WRITE TO ROMEO, AND HE WILL BE THERE WHEN YOU WAKE UP.

THEN YOU AND ROMEO CAN GO TO LIVE IN MANTUA.

I'LL DO IT! GOODBYE, FATHER.

JULIET RETURNED AT ONCE TO HER FATHER'S HOUSE.

FATHER, I MET PARIS IN FRIAR LAURENCE'S ROOM. I BELIEVE HE IS A GOOD MAN.

THEN YOU SHALL MARRY HIM TOMORROW INSTEAD OF THURSDAY!

UP IN HER ROOM, JULIET DRANK THE LIQUID FRIAR LAURENCE HAD GIVEN HER.

ROMEO, I DO THIS TO JOIN YOU!

WITHIN SECONDS, THE LIQUID HAD DONE ITS WORK.

THE NEXT MORNING, THE NURSE WENT TO JULIET'S ROOM TO PREPARE HER FOR THE WEDDING.

JULIET? OH, NO! SHE IS DEAD!

HEARING THE NURSE'S CRIES, LORD AND LADY CAPULET RUSHED INTO THE ROOM.

DEATH HAS COME LIKE A FROST TO THIS SWEET FLOWER.

DOWNSTAIRS, THE COUNTY PARIS WAITED WITH FRIAR LAURENCE.

IS THE BRIDE READY TO GO TO CHURCH?

SHE WILL GO TO CHURCH AND NEVER RETURN. JULIET IS DEAD!

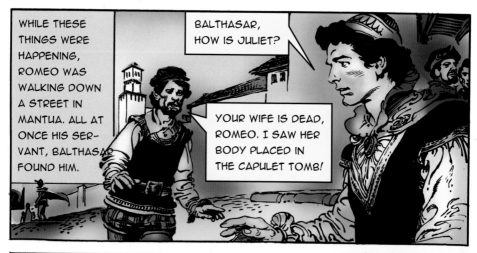

WHILE THESE THINGS WERE HAPPENING, ROMEO WAS WALKING DOWN A STREET IN MANTUA. ALL AT ONCE HIS SER-VANT, BALTHASAR FOUND HIM.

BALTHASAR, HOW IS JULIET?

YOUR WIFE IS DEAD, ROMEO. I SAW HER BODY PLACED IN THE CAPULET TOMB!

ROMEO WAS STUNNED AT THE NEWS, BUT HE MADE PLANS QUICKLY.

GET SOME HORSES FOR US, BALTHASAR. WE WILL LEAVE FOR VERONA TONIGHT. ARE THERE ANY MESSAGES FROM FRIAR LAURENCE?

NO, NONE.

WHEN BALTHASAR HAD GONE, ROMEO WENT TO A NEARBY DRUG STORE TO BUY SOME POISON. HE PLANNED TO TAKE HIS OWN LIFE AND DIE NEXT TO JULIET.

THIS IS ENOUGH TO KILL TWENTY MEN.

THANK YOU, SIR. HERE IS YOUR MONEY.

MEANWHILE, BACK IN VERONA, FRIAR LAURENCE WAS VERY UPSET. THE DAY BEFORE, HE HAD WRITTEN A LETTER TO ROMEO AND HAD GIVEN IT TO FRIAR JOHN. HE THOUGHT FRIAR JOHN WOULD BRING BACK AN ANSWER.

HAVE YOU BEEN TO SEE ROMEO, FRIAR JOHN?

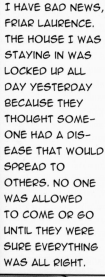

I HAVE BAD NEWS, FRIAR LAURENCE. THE HOUSE I WAS STAYING IN WAS LOCKED UP ALL DAY YESTERDAY BECAUSE THEY THOUGHT SOMEONE HAD A DISEASE THAT WOULD SPREAD TO OTHERS. NO ONE WAS ALLOWED TO COME OR GO UNTIL THEY WERE SURE EVERYTHING WAS ALL RIGHT.

THE LETTER YOU GAVE ME NEVER REACHED ROMEO.

WHAT? QUICK, GET ME SOME TOOLS! JULIET WILL WAKE UP IN THREE HOURS, AND ROMEO WON'T BE THERE!

AT THIS VERY MOMENT THE COUNTY PARIS WAS AT JULIET'S TOMB. SUDDENLY HIS SERVANT CALLED OUT TO HIM.

SIR, I HEAR HORSES COMING.

THEN I'LL STEP ASIDE FOR A MOMENT. I DON'T WANT ANYONE TO SEE ME.

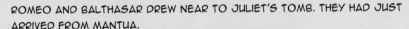

ROMEO AND BALTHASAR DREW NEAR TO JULIET'S TOMB. THEY HAD JUST ARRIVED FROM MANTUA.

TAKE THIS LETTER BALTHASAR, AND GIVE IT TO MY FATHER. I WOULD LIKE TO BE ALONE.

I WILL GO, SIR.

WHEN HE HAD GONE, ROMEO USED BALTHASAR'S TOOLS TO OPEN THE TOMB. SEEING THIS, PARIS STEPPED FROM THE SHADOWS AND ORDERED ROMEO TO STOP.

ROMEO, YOU KILLED JULIET'S COUSIN AND SHE DIED FROM SADNESS AT HIS DEATH. YOU MUST NOT DO ANYTHING ELSE TO HURT HER FAMILY. LEAVE HER TOMB ALONE.

ANYWAY, YOU MUST COME WITH ME TO THE PRINCE. BECAUSE YOU RETURNED TO VERONA, YOU WILL DIE!

YES, I WILL DIE, BUT I WILL DO IT MY OWN WAY. DO NOT TRY TO FORCE ME, OR I WILL HAVE TO FIGHT YOU!

BUT PARIS WOULD NOT LISTEN. THE TWO MEN FOUGHT, AND PARIS WAS KILLED.

SUDDENLY, ROMEO REALIZED THAT THE MAN HE HAD JUST KILLED WAS MERCUTIO'S COUSIN. MERCUTIO HAD BEEN ONE OF ROMEO'S BEST FRIENDS.

NOW I KNOW WHO THIS YOUNG MAN WAS.

I WILL LAY HIM IN THE TOMB NEAR JULIET. THEN I WILL JOIN THEM MYSELF!

SAYING THIS, ROMEO PICKED UP THE BODY OF PARIS AND WALKED INTO THE TOMB.

THEN HE DRANK THE BOTTLE OF POISON.

JUST BEFORE HE FELL, HE KISSED JULIET ONE LAST TIME.

GOODBYE, MY LOVE!

MOMENTS LATER, FRIAR LAURENCE AND BALTHASAR ENTERED THE TOMB. JULIET HAD JUST AWAKENED.

WHERE IS ROMEO?

HE IS DEAD, JULIET, AND SO IS PARIS. LET US GET OUT OF HERE AT ONCE!

BUT JULIET WAS TOO SHOCKED AND SAD TO LEAVE. MEANWHILE, FRIAR LAURENCE WAS AFRAID TO BE FOUND BY THE GUARDS, AND HE AND BALTHASAR LEFT QUICKLY.

I CANNOT LIVE WITHOUT ROMEO, SO I, TOO, MUST DIE!

WITH THIS, SHE TOOK ROMEO'S DAGGER AND PLUNGED IT INTO HER HEART.

CALLED BY PARIS' SERVANT, SEVERAL GUARDS SOON ARRIVED AT THE TOMB. ANOTHER GUARD BROUGHT BALTHASAR AND FRIAR LAURENCE BACK.

THERE IS A LOT OF BLOOD HERE. WHAT COULD HAVE HAPPENED?

ONE OF THE GUARDS WENT INTO THE TOMB AND FOUND THE BODIES. MEAN-WHILE, PRINCE ESCALUS AND THE CAPULETS ARRIVED.

ROMEO AND PARIS ARE DEAD. AND JULIET, WHO WE THOUGHT WAS DEAD BEFORE, SEEMS TO HAVE KILLED HERSELF!

BALTHASAR AND FRIAR LAURENCE WERE BROUGHT FORWARD FOR QUESTIONING JUST AS LORD MONTAGUE REACHED THE TOMB.

I WILL TELL YOU WHAT HAPPENED HERE, PRINCE ESCALUS. I SECRETLY MARRIED ROMEO AND JULIET.

I TRIED TO SAVE JULIET FROM A SECOND MAR-RIAGE BY HAVING HER PRETEND TO BE DEAD. ROMEO WAS TO HAVE TAKEN HER WITH HIM TO MANTUA. THESE DEATHS ARE ALL MY FAULT.

I FORGIVE YOU, FRIAR. YOU ONLY DID WHAT YOU THOUGHT BEST.

AT THAT BALTHASAR HANDED PRINCE ESCALUS THE LETTER ROMEO HAD GIVEN HIM. IT PROVED WHAT FRIAR LAURENCE HAD SAID WAS TRUE.

YOU MONTAGUES AND CAPULETS! SEE WHAT YOUR FIGHTING HAS DONE? FIRST OF ALL, MERCUTIO AND PARIS ARE DEAD.

THE CAPULETS HAVE LOST JULIET AND THE MONTAGUES HAVE LOST ROMEO. ALL OF US HAVE BEEN PUNISHED BECAUSE OF YOU!

AND FINALLY, AT THE PRINCE'S WORDS, THE TWO FAMILIES REALIZED HOW STUPID THEY HAD BEEN.

MONTAGUE, GIVE ME YOUR HAND. FROM THIS DAY FORTH OUR FEUD IS OVER!

I GIVE YOU MY HAND AND MORE. WE SHALL NEVER FIGHT AGAIN!

THAT IS GOOD! BUT FOR NOW, LET US LEAVE THIS PLACE. THE SAD STORY OF WHAT HAPPENED HERE WILL REMAIN WITH US ALWAYS!

END